DARK PASSING

Copyright © 2024 by Linda Carrol. All rights reserved worldwide. No part of this publication may be replicated, redistributed, or given away in any form without the prior written consent of the author/publisher or the terms relayed to you herein.

Kindred Souls Press
Baytown, Texas 77520

Prologue

Dark Passing is a tale of suspense, secrets, and the relentless pursuit of truth. Set in the small, seemingly tranquil town of Pinewood, the story follows Emma Collins, a tenacious young journalist with an unyielding drive to uncover the truth. Pinewood, with its quiet streets and friendly faces, hides a dark history that begins to resurface when a mysterious stranger arrives in town.

Emma has always felt that Pinewood had its share of secrets, but nothing could have prepared her for the chilling events that begin to unfold. It all starts with a peculiar letter left on her doorstep, hinting at a hidden past that no one in town wants to talk about. Intrigued and unnerved, Emma starts her investigation, only to find herself entangled in a web of lies and danger.

As Emma delves deeper, she discovers a secret room in an old, abandoned mansion on the outskirts of town. The room holds clues to a decades-old mystery involving the town's most respected citizens. The deeper she digs, the more she realizes that the past is not as buried as she once thought. Shadows lurk around every corner, and the more she uncovers, the more she puts herself and those she loves at risk.

In "Dark Passing," every clue brings Emma closer to the truth but also closer to danger. She finds herself in a race against time to piece together the puzzle before it's too late. Along the way, she must navigate treacherous alliances, face betrayal from unexpected quarters, and confront the dark forces that have kept Pinewood's secrets hidden for so long.

The story is filled with twists and turns, keeping readers on the edge of their seats. As Emma fights to bring the truth to light, she learns that some secrets are meant to stay buried, and some truths can shatter lives. "Dark Passing" is a gripping mystery that explores the lengths to which people will go to protect their secrets and the courage it takes to uncover the truth.

Chapter 1: The Mysterious Arrival

Emma Collins sat at her desk in the Pinewood Gazette, tapping her pen against the notepad in front of her. The newsroom was quiet, the only sound the hum of computers and the occasional ring of a phone. It was a slow news day in Pinewood, and Emma was itching for a story, something that would break the monotony of local council meetings and school events.

Her thoughts were interrupted by the creak of the front door. She looked up to see a tall figure silhouetted against the bright afternoon sun. The stranger stepped inside, letting the door close softly behind him. He was dressed in a long, dark coat, his face partially obscured by a wide-brimmed hat. Emma's curiosity was piqued. Pinewood didn't get many visitors, especially not ones who looked like they'd stepped out of a noir film.

The man approached the front desk where Jane, the receptionist, greeted him. Emma couldn't hear their conversation, but she noticed Jane's eyes widen in surprise before she pointed in Emma's direction. The stranger nodded and made his way over, each step deliberate and measured.

"Miss Collins?" he asked, his voice smooth but with an edge that made Emma sit up straighter.

"Yes, I'm Emma Collins. How can I help you?"

He reached into his coat and pulled out a small, weathered envelope. "I believe this might interest you," he said, handing it to her.

Emma took the envelope, noting the old-fashioned wax seal stamped with an intricate emblem she didn't recognize. She glanced up to ask the stranger about it, but he was already heading toward the door.

"Wait!" she called out. "Who are you?"

The man paused, turning his head slightly. "Just a messenger," he replied before disappearing into the sunlight.

Emma looked down at the envelope in her hands, her heart racing with anticipation. She broke the seal and unfolded the letter inside. The handwriting was elegant, almost too perfect, and the words sent a shiver down her spine.

"Secrets lie buried in Pinewood. The past is never truly gone. Follow the clues and uncover the truth, or darkness will consume us all."

Emma's mind raced with questions. Who had sent this letter? What secrets were buried in Pinewood? And why had they chosen her to uncover them? She knew one thing for certain: this was the story she'd been waiting for.

She grabbed her notepad and pen, ready to follow the trail, wherever it might lead. Little did she know, the mysterious arrival was just the beginning of a journey that would change her life—and Pinewood—forever.

Chapter 2: The First Clue

Emma couldn't shake the feeling of unease as she re-read the letter. The words seemed to echo in her mind, urging her to delve deeper into Pinewood's hidden past. She carefully folded the letter and slipped it into her notebook, resolving to find out more about the mysterious message.

The newsroom remained quiet as Emma scanned the shelves for any old records that might provide a starting point. Pinewood was a town with a long history, and somewhere within its archives lay the key to unlocking the mystery.

"Hey, Emma," called out Sam, the Gazette's photographer, breaking her concentration. "What are you up to?"

Emma considered sharing the letter but decided against it. "Just looking into some old town history," she replied casually. "Thought there might be a story here."

Sam raised an eyebrow but didn't press further. "Let me know if you need any photos," he said before returning to his desk.

Emma's search yielded nothing unusual until she came across an old, dusty ledger marked "Pinewood Historical Society." Flipping through the pages, she found a reference to a significant event that had taken place in the town nearly a century ago: the mysterious disappearance of a prominent family, the Aldens.

Intrigued, Emma took out her notepad and jotted down key details. The Alden family had been well-known in Pinewood, owning a large estate on the outskirts of town. One night, they vanished without a trace, leaving behind a mansion full of unanswered questions. The case had been a sensation at the time, but with no leads, it eventually faded from memory.

Emma decided to visit the old Alden mansion, now abandoned and rumored to be haunted. She packed her camera, flashlight, and the notebook containing the letter and set out for the outskirts of Pinewood.

The mansion stood at the end of a long, overgrown driveway, shrouded in shadows cast by ancient trees. Emma felt a chill as she approached the imposing structure. The house had an eerie beauty, its grandeur diminished by years of neglect. She pushed open the creaky gate and made her way to the front door, which stood slightly ajar.

Taking a deep breath, Emma stepped inside. The interior was just as she imagined—dusty, dark, and filled with relics of a bygone era. She swept her flashlight across the foyer, revealing a grand staircase and a hallway lined with portraits of stern-looking ancestors. The air was thick with the scent of decay, and the silence was almost deafening.

Emma began her search, exploring each room methodically. She found little more than old furniture and cobwebs until she entered what appeared to be the study. The room was lined with bookshelves, and a large oak desk dominated the center. On the desk, she noticed an old, leather-bound journal. She carefully opened it, hoping to find some clue about the Alden family's disappearance.

The journal belonged to Richard Alden, the patriarch of the family. His entries detailed their daily lives, his business dealings, and, most intriguingly, his increasing paranoia. The final entries were fragmented and cryptic, mentioning a "dark presence" and a "hidden truth" that must never be revealed.

Emma's heart raced as she read the last entry:

"We are not alone. The shadows watch, waiting. I fear for my family's safety. If anything happens to us, the secret must be kept hidden. The key lies beneath."

Beneath what? Emma wondered. She searched the study for any hidden compartments but found nothing. Frustrated, she decided to check the basement, suspecting it might hold more answers.

The basement door was heavy and groaned as Emma pushed it open. The stairs creaked under her weight, and the air grew colder the deeper she descended. She reached the bottom and shone her flashlight around, revealing a dank, musty room filled with old crates and broken furniture.

Emma's flashlight beam caught something shiny on the far wall—a small, metallic keyhole embedded in the stone. She approached it, feeling a surge of excitement. Could this be what Richard Alden's journal referred to?

She searched the basement for the key but found nothing. Determined, she returned to the study, hoping she had overlooked something. After a thorough search, she found a small, ornate key hidden inside a hollowed-out book on the shelf.

Her hands trembled with anticipation as she returned to the basement. She inserted the key into the keyhole, and with a click, a hidden door swung open, revealing a narrow passageway.

Emma's flashlight flickered as she stepped inside, her heart pounding. The passageway led to a small, hidden room containing a single wooden chest. She opened the chest, revealing a collection of old documents and photographs. Among them was a letter, much like the one she had received, warning of the dangers of uncovering the past.

Emma felt a shiver run down her spine. Someone had gone to great lengths to hide these secrets, and she was now in the midst of something far bigger than she had imagined. The pieces of the puzzle were starting to come together, but she knew there was still much to uncover.

As she carefully placed the documents back in the chest, Emma knew one thing for certain: the mystery of the Alden family's disappearance was only the beginning. Dark forces were at play, and she was determined to bring the truth to light, no matter the cost.

Emma emerged from the mansion with a renewed sense of purpose. The first clue had led her to a hidden room and a chest full of secrets, but there were still many unanswered questions. Who had sent her the letter? What dark presence had Richard Alden feared? And what did it have to do with the present day?

As she made her way back to town, Emma felt the weight of the mystery pressing down on her. She had taken the first step on a dangerous path, but there was no turning back now. Pinewood's secrets were calling to her, and she was determined to uncover them, one clue at a time.

With a new sense of determination, Emma prepared herself for the challenges ahead. The shadows of Pinewood were deep and filled with secrets, but she was ready to face them. The journey had just begun, and Emma Collins was not one to back down from a mystery.

Chapter 3: Stranger in the Shadows

Emma couldn't shake the unsettling feeling as she left the Alden mansion. The old house had given her a crucial piece of the puzzle, but the hidden room and the ominous letter inside the chest had raised more questions than answers. Determined to uncover the truth, she returned to her apartment and spread out the documents on her kitchen table.

The photographs were faded, but one stood out. It was a picture of the Alden family, taken in front of the mansion. Richard Alden stood tall and proud, his arm around his wife, Eleanor. Their children, Thomas and Lillian, smiled innocently at the camera. But in the background, half-hidden in the shadows, was a figure Emma hadn't noticed before. A man, his face obscured, watching the family with an intensity that sent a chill down her spine.

Who was this man? Could he be the dark presence Richard had written about? Emma's mind raced with possibilities. She needed more information and knew just the place to get it.

The next morning, Emma visited the Pinewood Historical Society. The building, a quaint cottage surrounded by well-tended gardens, was run by Mrs. Edith Hargrave, a lifelong resident of Pinewood and the town's unofficial historian.

"Good morning, Mrs. Hargrave," Emma greeted as she entered the small office.

"Emma, dear! What brings you here today?" Mrs. Hargrave asked, her eyes twinkling behind her glasses.

"I'm doing some research on the Alden family," Emma replied, trying to sound casual. "I found an old journal that mentioned them, and it piqued my curiosity."

Mrs. Hargrave's expression shifted to one of concern. "The Aldens... That was a dark chapter in Pinewood's history. Such a tragedy."

Emma nodded. "I was hoping you might have some records or photos that could help me understand what happened to them."

Mrs. Hargrave sighed, then stood and walked to a large filing cabinet. She rummaged through the drawers before pulling out a thick file. "These are all the records we have on the Aldens. It's not much, but it might help."

Emma thanked her and sat down to review the file. There were newspaper clippings, legal documents, and more photographs. As she sifted through the information, a name kept appearing: Henry Whitaker, the family's long-time lawyer and confidant. According to the documents, Whitaker had been deeply involved in the Aldens' affairs, both personal and financial.

Emma's heart skipped a beat when she found a photograph of Henry Whitaker. He was the same man from the background of the family photo, the one watching the Aldens with such intensity. Could he be the dark presence Richard Alden had feared?

With a new lead to follow, Emma left the Historical Society and headed to the town's archives, hoping to find more about Henry Whitaker. The archives were housed in the basement of the town hall, a dimly lit room filled with rows of filing cabinets and shelves laden with old documents.

After hours of searching, Emma found what she was looking for. Henry Whitaker had been a prominent figure in Pinewood, but his reputation was marred by rumors and scandal. There were whispers of shady business dealings, blackmail, and even a connection to organized crime. His sudden disappearance shortly after the Alden family's was never explained, adding another layer to the mystery.

Emma's mind raced as she pieced together the information. Whitaker had been close to the Aldens, but his motives were unclear. Had he betrayed them? Or had he been protecting them from something even darker?

As she left the archives, Emma felt the weight of the mystery pressing down on her. She needed to talk to someone who might have more insight into Henry Whitaker's relationship with the Aldens. There was only one person left in Pinewood who might know: Margaret Harris, the former housekeeper of the Alden family.

Margaret lived in a small cottage on the edge of town. Emma drove there, hoping the elderly woman could shed some light on the dark events of the past. She knocked on the door, and after a moment, it opened to reveal a frail but sharp-eyed woman.

"Mrs. Harris? My name is Emma Collins. I'm a journalist with the Pinewood Gazette. I was hoping you could tell me about the Alden family."

Margaret's eyes narrowed. "The Aldens? That was a long time ago. Why dig up the past?"

Emma hesitated, then showed Margaret the letter she had received and explained her investigation. The old woman's expression softened, and she nodded slowly. "Come in, then. We have much to talk about."

Inside, the cottage was cozy and filled with the scent of fresh-baked bread. Emma sat at the kitchen table while Margaret poured them both a cup of tea. The old woman sighed as she settled into her chair.

"The Aldens were good people," Margaret began. "But they had secrets, as all families do. Henry Whitaker was more than their lawyer; he was like a member of the family. But something changed in him towards the end. He became secretive, always meeting with strangers late at night. Mr. Alden started to suspect him of... something. He never told me what, but it weighed heavily on him."

Emma leaned forward, hanging on Margaret's every word. "Do you know what might have caused Richard Alden's paranoia?"

Margaret shook her head. "I don't, but I do remember the night they disappeared. There was a storm, and the power went out. I heard voices arguing downstairs, and when I went to check, I saw Mr. Whitaker leaving the house. He looked... different, almost frightened. That was the last time I saw any of them."

Emma's mind whirled with possibilities. "Do you think Whitaker had something to do with their disappearance?"

"I don't know, dear," Margaret said, her voice trembling. "But whatever it was, it was something dark. Something that shouldn't be disturbed."

Emma thanked Margaret for her time and left the cottage, her thoughts a jumble of theories and suspicions. The mystery of the Alden family was deepening, and the shadows that had haunted Pinewood for so long were starting to take shape.

As she drove back to town, Emma noticed a figure standing in the distance, watching her. She couldn't make out the face, but the presence was unnerving. Was it Whitaker? Or someone else trying to keep the past buried?

Emma's heart pounded as she sped up, leaving the figure behind. She had to be careful; the more she uncovered, the more dangerous this investigation became. But she was determined to find the truth, no matter the cost.

The stranger in the shadows was a reminder that someone was watching, and they didn't want the secrets of Pinewood to be revealed. Emma's resolve hardened. She would not be intimidated. The darkness was closing in, but she was ready to face it head-on.

Chapter 4: A Hidden Past

The encounter with Margaret Harris had given Emma valuable insights, but it had also raised more questions. The Alden family's mysterious disappearance, Henry Whitaker's suspicious behavior, and the strange figure watching her from the shadows—all these elements were pieces of a larger puzzle that Emma was determined to solve.

Back in her apartment, Emma sat at her desk, surrounded by the documents and photographs she had collected. The letter, the journal, the old photographs—each item seemed to hold a part of the story, but she needed more to connect the dots. She decided to focus on Henry Whitaker. If he was as deeply involved as she suspected, his past might provide the answers she was looking for.

Emma started by searching through public records, hoping to find more about Whitaker's background. She discovered that he had grown up in Pinewood and had established himself as a successful lawyer in his early twenties. However, there was a gap in his records during his formative years, a period when he seemed to vanish from public life.

Curiosity piqued, Emma decided to visit the Pinewood Public Library to see if she could find any more information. The library was a quiet, old building, its wooden shelves lined with books that had seen better days. Emma made her way to the local history section and began her search.

After hours of digging through old newspapers and town records, Emma found an article from the late 1920s that mentioned a scandal involving Whitaker's family. His father, Thomas Whitaker, had been implicated in a major embezzlement scheme that had rocked Pinewood's financial community. The elder Whitaker had been arrested and subsequently disappeared under mysterious circumstances.

Emma's fingers trembled as she held the fragile newspaper clipping. Henry Whitaker had been a young boy when his father was accused. Could this family disgrace have shaped his later actions? Emma noted down the details and continued her research, hoping to find more connections.

As she delved deeper, she uncovered another surprising fact: Henry Whitaker had a sister, Alice, who had been sent away to live with relatives after their father's arrest. There was no further mention of her in the town records. Intrigued, Emma decided to follow this lead, hoping Alice Whitaker might still be alive and able to shed light on her brother's past.

Emma tracked down an address for Alice Whitaker in a neighboring town and set off the next morning. The drive was long and filled with anticipation. She had no idea what to expect but hoped that Alice could provide the missing pieces of the puzzle.

The address led her to a modest house in a quiet suburb. Emma parked her car and walked up to the front door, her heart pounding. She rang the bell and waited, rehearsing what she would say.

The door opened to reveal an elderly woman with sharp blue eyes and a kind smile. "Yes? Can I help you?"

"Ms. Whitaker? My name is Emma Collins. I'm a journalist from Pinewood. I'm investigating some events involving your brother, Henry, and the Alden family. May I speak with you?"

Alice Whitaker's expression shifted from curiosity to a guarded look. "Henry and the Aldens? That's a name I haven't heard in a long time. Come in."

Inside, the house was warm and inviting, filled with family photos and memorabilia. Alice led Emma to the living room and gestured for her to sit. "I suppose you're here about what happened all those years ago."

Emma nodded. "Yes, Ms. Whitaker. I'm trying to piece together what happened to the Alden family, and it seems your brother was involved. Can you tell me more about him and your family?"

Alice sighed, her eyes distant with memory. "Henry was always a troubled soul. After our father's scandal, our family was never the same. Henry took it the hardest. He was determined to restore our family's honor, no matter the cost. He became obsessed with power and influence, often associating with dangerous people."

"Do you think he had something to do with the Alden family's disappearance?" Emma asked gently.

Alice hesitated, then nodded slowly. "Henry was deeply involved with Richard Alden. They were friends once, but something changed. Henry started acting strangely, talking about secrets that couldn't be revealed. He became paranoid, always looking over his shoulder."

Emma leaned forward. "Do you know what these secrets were?"

Alice shook her head. "I don't know the specifics. Henry kept those things to himself. But I do know he was involved in something dark. After the Aldens disappeared, Henry vanished too. I never saw him again."

Emma felt a chill. "Do you think he's still alive?"

Alice's eyes were sad. "I don't know. But if he is, he's not the man I knew. Whatever he was involved in, it changed him. Consumed him."

Emma thanked Alice for her time and the valuable information. As she drove back to Pinewood, her mind raced with new theories. Henry Whitaker's obsession with power, his connection to the Aldens, and the dark secrets he carried were all pieces of a larger, more sinister puzzle.

Back in Pinewood, Emma reviewed her notes. Henry Whitaker had been close to the Aldens, but his motives were still unclear. The next step was to find out more about his connections and the people he had associated with. Someone in Pinewood must know more about the events that had transpired.

Emma decided to visit Sheriff Tom Harris, who had been a deputy at the time of the Alden family's disappearance. He might have insights that could help her make sense of the information she had gathered.

The Pinewood Sheriff's Office was a small, unassuming building. Emma walked in, feeling a mixture of hope and apprehension. She approached the front desk, where a young deputy greeted her.

"I'm here to see Sheriff Harris. My name is Emma Collins. I'm investigating the Alden family's disappearance."

The deputy nodded and led her to the sheriff's office. Sheriff Tom Harris was a tall, imposing man in his sixties, with a stern but kind face. He looked up from his desk as Emma entered.

"Ms. Collins, I've heard about your investigation. What can I do for you?"

Emma explained her research and the information she had uncovered about Henry Whitaker. Sheriff Harris listened intently, his expression growing more serious with each detail.

"Henry Whitaker was always a person of interest in the Alden case," the sheriff said finally. "But we could never find enough evidence to link him directly to their disappearance. He was a slippery one, always covering his tracks."

"Do you think he's still alive?" Emma asked.

Sheriff Harris shrugged. "It's possible. If anyone could disappear without a trace, it would be him. But there were always rumors about his involvement with some unsavory characters. Organized crime, secret societies—things that were hard to prove but always seemed to linger in the background."

Emma felt a sense of urgency. "Do you have any leads or contacts that might help me find out more about his connections?"

The sheriff thought for a moment, then nodded. "There was a man, a private investigator named Jack Monroe. He was hired by the Aldens to look into some threats they were receiving before they disappeared. He might have some information. Last I heard, he was living in the next town over."

Emma thanked Sheriff Harris and left the office, feeling a renewed sense of purpose. She had a new lead and was determined to follow it. The shadows of Pinewood's past were starting to clear, and she was getting closer to the truth.

As she drove to meet Jack Monroe, Emma couldn't shake the feeling of being watched. The figure in the shadows, the dark presence that seemed to follow her—it was all connected. She had to stay vigilant and trust no one.

The road ahead was dangerous, but Emma was ready. The hidden past of Pinewood was slowly being revealed, and she was determined to uncover the secrets that had been buried for so long. The truth was out there, waiting to be found, and Emma Collins would not rest until she had brought it to light.

Chapter 5: Whispers in the Night

The drive to the neighboring town gave Emma time to think. Jack Monroe, the private investigator hired by the Aldens, might be the key to unraveling the mystery. She had to remain focused and cautious; this investigation was becoming more dangerous with each step she took.

Jack Monroe's address led her to a modest house on the outskirts of the neighboring town. The house was neat, with a well-kept lawn and a porch swing that creaked in the breeze. Emma parked her car and walked up to the front door, taking a deep breath before knocking.

The door opened to reveal a man in his late sixties, his sharp eyes and rugged demeanor hinting at a life spent uncovering secrets. "Can I help you?" he asked, his voice gruff but not unfriendly.

"Mr. Monroe? My name is Emma Collins. I'm a journalist from Pinewood, investigating the disappearance of the Alden family. I was told you might have information that could help me."

Jack Monroe studied her for a moment before nodding. "Come in, Ms. Collins."

Inside, the house was filled with mementos of Monroe's career—photographs, newspaper clippings, and framed certificates adorned the walls. He led Emma to a small study, where they sat opposite each other at a cluttered desk.

"I haven't thought about the Aldens in years," Monroe began, his tone reflective. "That case haunted me for a long time."

Emma leaned forward, her notebook ready. "Can you tell me what you found during your investigation?"

Monroe nodded. "Richard Alden hired me after they started receiving threats. Anonymous letters, phone calls in the middle of the night—typical intimidation tactics. He was convinced someone was trying to drive them out of Pinewood."

"Did he have any idea who might be behind it?" Emma asked.

"He suspected Henry Whitaker," Monroe replied. "They were friends once, but something had soured between them. Richard believed Henry was involved in something illegal, something that put the entire family at risk."

Emma's heart raced. "What kind of illegal activities?"

"Whitaker was involved with some dangerous people," Monroe said, his expression darkening. "Organized crime, secret societies—things that were hard to prove but very real. Richard wanted to confront him, but before he could, the family disappeared."

Emma took a deep breath. "Do you think Whitaker was responsible for their disappearance?"

Monroe hesitated. "I think he knew more than he let on. But without concrete evidence, it was all speculation. After the Aldens vanished, Whitaker went underground. I couldn't track him down."

"Do you think he's still alive?" Emma asked.

"Hard to say," Monroe replied. "If he is, he's well-hidden. But someone with his connections doesn't just disappear without a trace."

Emma thanked Monroe for his time and information. As she left his house, she felt a mix of hope and frustration. She was getting closer to the truth, but the more she uncovered, the more dangerous the situation became.

Back in Pinewood, Emma decided to visit the Alden mansion again. There was something about the house that called to her, as if it held more secrets waiting to be discovered. She packed her camera, flashlight, and notebook, and set off for the mansion.

The sun was setting as Emma arrived at the old estate. The mansion loomed in the twilight, its windows dark and foreboding. She made her way inside, the creaking floorboards echoing in the silence. She headed straight for the hidden room in the basement, hoping to find more clues.

As she descended the stairs, Emma heard a faint whispering sound. She paused, straining to hear. The whispers grew louder, a chorus of voices speaking in hushed tones. Her heart pounded as she reached the bottom of the stairs and shone her flashlight around the room.

The whispers seemed to emanate from the walls themselves, filling the air with an eerie presence. Emma felt a shiver run down her spine. She approached the wooden chest she had found earlier and opened it, hoping to find something she had missed.

Inside the chest, she found an old, tattered diary. The cover was worn, and the pages were yellowed with age. Emma carefully opened it, her eyes scanning the handwritten entries. The diary belonged to Eleanor Alden, and her words painted a chilling picture of the family's final days.

Eleanor wrote of her husband's growing paranoia, the threats they had received, and their fear of Henry Whitaker. She described strange occurrences in the house—whispers in the night, shadows that seemed to move on their own, and a sense of being watched. Her final entries were filled with despair, as she feared for her family's safety.

Emma's hands trembled as she read Eleanor's last entry: "Richard is convinced that Henry is behind the threats. He plans to confront him tonight. I pray that we are safe, but the darkness is closing in. If something happens to us, may these words serve as a warning. The truth must be uncovered, no matter the cost."

Emma closed the diary, her mind racing. Eleanor's words confirmed her suspicions. Henry Whitaker was involved, and the threats were real. But the whispers in the house, the feeling of being watched—what did they mean? Was there something more to this mystery than she had imagined?

As Emma prepared to leave, she heard footsteps above her. She froze, her heart pounding. Someone was in the house. She quickly turned off her flashlight and hid behind a stack of old crates, hoping to remain unseen.

The footsteps grew louder, descending the stairs. Emma held her breath, peeking through a gap in the crates. A figure appeared in the doorway, their face obscured by the shadows. They moved slowly, methodically, as if searching for something.

Emma's mind raced. Who was this person? Were they looking for her? She stayed as still as possible, barely daring to breathe. The figure approached the chest and opened it, rifling through the contents. Emma's heart pounded in her chest, each beat echoing in the silence.

After what felt like an eternity, the figure closed the chest and stood up. They turned and left the room, their footsteps fading as they ascended the stairs. Emma waited a few moments before cautiously emerging from her hiding place.

She quickly made her way out of the mansion, her mind reeling. Someone else was searching for the same answers she was, and they were willing to go to great lengths to find them. The danger was real, and she had to be more careful than ever.

Back in her apartment, Emma reviewed her notes. The diary, the whispers, the mysterious figure in the mansion—all of it pointed to a larger conspiracy. She was determined to uncover the truth, but she knew she couldn't do it alone.

Emma decided to enlist the help of Sam, the Gazette's photographer and her closest friend. She needed someone she could trust, someone who could watch her back as she delved deeper into the mystery.

The next morning, Emma met Sam at the Gazette's office. She explained everything she had discovered, from the letter to the hidden room, the diary, and the mysterious figure in the mansion.

Sam listened intently, his expression growing more serious with each detail. "This is big, Emma. Are you sure you want to keep digging? It sounds dangerous."

"I don't have a choice," Emma replied. "The truth needs to be uncovered, and I can't do it alone. Will you help me?"

Sam nodded. "Of course. Whatever it takes."

With Sam's support, Emma felt a renewed sense of determination. They were in this together, and she was ready to face whatever dangers lay ahead. The whispers in the night were growing louder, but Emma Collins was not afraid.

The mystery of the Alden family was unraveling, and she was getting closer to the truth. But the darkness was also closing in, and Emma knew she had to be prepared for anything. The shadows of Pinewood held many secrets, and she was determined to uncover them all, no matter the cost.

Chapter 6: The Secret Room

With Sam by her side, Emma felt more confident in her investigation. The diary, the whispers, and the mysterious figure in the mansion were all signs that she was on the right track, but also that danger was closing in. They decided to revisit the Alden mansion together, hoping to uncover more clues and confront whatever or whoever was watching them.

As they drove to the mansion, the sky was overcast, casting a somber mood over their journey. The mansion loomed in the distance, its windows dark and foreboding. Emma and Sam parked the car and made their way to the front door, each step filled with anticipation.

The interior was just as eerie as Emma remembered. The silence was almost palpable, broken only by the creaking floorboards beneath their feet. They headed straight for the basement, where Emma had found the hidden room and the chest.

"Stay close," Emma whispered to Sam as they descended the stairs. "We don't know who's watching."

In the basement, Emma showed Sam the hidden room and the chest. They examined the documents again, but nothing new stood out. Then, Sam noticed something Emma had missed before—a small, almost invisible latch on the floor next to the chest.

"What's this?" Sam asked, pointing to the latch.

Emma's heart raced as she knelt to examine it. The latch was cleverly concealed, blending seamlessly with the floorboards. She carefully lifted it, revealing a hidden compartment beneath the floor. Inside, they found an old, leather-bound book and a set of keys.

Emma opened the book, her eyes widening as she read the title: "The Alden Family Secrets." The book was a ledger, detailing the family's financial transactions, business dealings, and personal secrets. As she flipped through the pages, she found entries that confirmed Richard Alden's suspicions about Henry Whitaker.

"Look at this," Emma said, showing Sam a page detailing large sums of money transferred to Whitaker from accounts linked to organized crime. "This proves Whitaker was involved in illegal activities."

Sam nodded. "But why did Richard keep this hidden? What was he afraid of?"

Emma continued reading, finding more entries about secret meetings, threats, and a growing sense of paranoia. The final entry was chilling: "Whitaker knows. We are not safe. The truth must be protected at all costs. The key lies with Eleanor."

Emma's mind raced. What key? And what did Eleanor know that was so important?

They examined the set of keys they had found with the book. There were three keys, each labeled with a different room in the mansion: the study, the master bedroom, and the attic.

"Let's start with the study," Emma said, holding up the key. "Maybe we'll find more answers there."

They made their way to the study, the room where Emma had found Richard Alden's journal. She unlocked the door and they stepped inside, their flashlights illuminating the dust-covered furniture and bookshelves. They searched the room thoroughly, but found nothing new.

Next, they headed to the master bedroom. Emma used the second key to unlock the door. The room was opulent, with a large four-poster bed, antique furniture, and ornate decorations. They searched the room, finding only old clothes and personal items. Then Sam noticed a small, locked drawer in the nightstand.

"Try the last key," Sam suggested.

Emma unlocked the drawer, revealing a small metal box. Inside was a stack of letters, tied together with a faded ribbon. Emma carefully untied the ribbon and began reading the letters. They were from Eleanor to Richard, written in the weeks leading up to their disappearance. The letters detailed Eleanor's growing fear of Henry Whitaker and her suspicions that he was planning something terrible.

"Eleanor was scared," Emma said, her voice trembling. "She knew something was going to happen, but Richard didn't believe her."

Sam placed a comforting hand on her shoulder. "We'll find the truth, Emma. We're getting closer."

The last letter was the most revealing. Eleanor wrote about a secret room in the attic, a place where Richard had hidden something important. Emma's heart raced as she read the final lines: "If anything happens to us, the key is hidden with my most precious possession."

Emma and Sam exchanged a glance. "The attic," Emma said. "We need to find that key."

They climbed the narrow stairs to the attic, the air growing colder with each step. The attic was dark and filled with old furniture, trunks, and forgotten memories. Emma used the last key to unlock the attic door, and they stepped inside.

They searched the attic, but there was no sign of the key. Frustration began to set in until Emma remembered Eleanor's words: "my most precious possession." She thought about the letters, about Eleanor's love for her family. What could be more precious than that?

Emma's eyes fell on an old, ornate music box on a shelf. She carefully picked it up and opened it. The haunting melody filled the air as a small ballerina twirled inside. Beneath the ballerina was a hidden compartment, and inside it, a small, brass key.

"This must be it," Emma said, holding up the key.

They searched the attic for any hidden doors or compartments. In the far corner, behind a stack of old trunks, they found a small, concealed door. Emma used the brass key to unlock it, revealing a hidden room.

The room was small and dark, filled with old books, documents, and a large, wooden chest. Emma's hands trembled as she opened the chest, revealing a collection of artifacts and papers. At the bottom of the chest was a metal box, locked and heavy.

Emma used the brass key to unlock the metal box. Inside, she found a stack of documents labeled "The Whitaker Conspiracy." The documents detailed Whitaker's illegal activities, his connections to organized crime, and his plans to take over the Alden family's business empire.

"This is it," Emma said, her voice filled with awe. "This is the proof we need."

Sam nodded. "We need to get this to the authorities. Whitaker's crimes can't stay hidden any longer."

As they prepared to leave the attic, Emma heard the whispers again, louder and more insistent. She felt a chill run down her spine as she realized they were not alone. Someone was watching them, waiting for the right moment to strike.

"We need to get out of here," Emma whispered to Sam. "Now."

They quickly made their way down the stairs, the whispers growing louder with each step. As they reached the front door, they heard footsteps behind them. Emma turned to see a figure emerging from the shadows, their face hidden beneath a hood.

"Go!" Emma shouted to Sam, pushing him toward the door.

They ran to the car, the figure chasing them. Emma fumbled with the keys, finally managing to unlock the car. They jumped in and sped away, the figure disappearing into the darkness behind them.

Emma's heart pounded as they drove back to Pinewood. They had the proof they needed, but the danger was far from over. Someone wanted to keep the Whitaker conspiracy hidden, and they were willing to go to any lengths to do so.

As they reached the safety of Emma's apartment, she felt a sense of relief mixed with dread. The truth was within their grasp, but the shadows of Pinewood were closing in. They had to act quickly, before it was too late.

With Sam's help, Emma prepared the documents for the authorities. They knew they had to be careful; whoever was behind the conspiracy would not give up easily. The secret room had revealed the truth, but the real battle was just beginning.

The darkness was closing in, but Emma Collins was ready to face it head-on. The mystery of the Alden family was unraveling, and she was determined to bring the truth to light, no matter the cost.

Chapter 7: Unraveling the Truth

Emma and Sam spent the night poring over the documents they had found in the Alden mansion. The more they read, the clearer the picture became: Henry Whitaker had been involved in a vast network of illegal activities, using the Alden family's resources to cover his tracks. The evidence they had was damning, but they needed to present it carefully to avoid tipping off anyone who might still be loyal to Whitaker.

The next morning, they decided to visit Sheriff Harris again, this time with the full story. Emma felt a mix of excitement and apprehension as they walked into the Pinewood Sheriff's Office. They were greeted by the same young deputy, who led them to the sheriff's office.

Sheriff Harris looked up from his desk as they entered, his eyes narrowing as he saw the stack of documents in Emma's hands. "Ms. Collins, Mr. Johnson, what do you have for me?"

Emma took a deep breath and began to explain everything, from the initial letter to the hidden room in the Alden mansion and the documents they had found. Sheriff Harris listened intently, his expression growing more serious with each passing moment.

When Emma finished, she handed the documents to the sheriff. "This is the proof we've been looking for. Whitaker was behind the threats to the Alden family, and he used their resources to cover up his illegal activities."

Sheriff Harris flipped through the documents, his brow furrowing. "This is substantial evidence. If what you're saying is true, we have a strong case against Whitaker and anyone involved with him."

Emma nodded. "But we need to be careful. Someone tried to stop us last night at the mansion. They know we're getting close."

The sheriff's expression hardened. "I'll assign a team to investigate this further. We'll keep this under wraps until we have enough to make arrests. In the meantime, you both need to be careful. If Whitaker or his associates suspect anything, they won't hesitate to take action."

Emma and Sam left the sheriff's office feeling a mix of relief and anxiety. They had taken a significant step towards uncovering the truth, but they were also more vulnerable than ever. They decided to lay low for a while, avoiding unnecessary risks until the investigation gained more traction.

That night, Emma couldn't sleep. Her mind kept replaying the events of the past few days, the pieces of the puzzle slowly falling into place. She knew they were on the right track, but the danger was real and ever-present.

The next morning, Emma received a call from Sheriff Harris. "We've made some progress," he said. "I need you and Sam to come down to the office. There's something you need to see."

Emma and Sam hurried to the sheriff's office, their hearts pounding with anticipation. When they arrived, Sheriff Harris led them to a conference room where several deputies were gathered around a table covered with maps and photographs.

"We've identified several of Whitaker's associates," Sheriff Harris explained, pointing to the photographs. "They've been involved in various illegal activities, from money laundering to intimidation. We're building a case against them, but we need more concrete evidence to make arrests."

Emma studied the photographs, recognizing some of the faces from the documents they had found. "What can we do to help?"

Sheriff Harris handed her a file. "There's one person who might have the information we need. His name is Michael Turner. He used to be Whitaker's right-hand man, but they had a falling out a few years ago. If anyone knows Whitaker's secrets, it's him."

Emma and Sam exchanged a glance. "Where can we find him?" Sam asked.

"He's been living off the grid since the fallout," Sheriff Harris replied. "But we've tracked him to a cabin in the woods outside of town. It's risky, but if you can get him to talk, we might have enough to bring Whitaker and his associates down."

Emma nodded, determination in her eyes. "We'll do it."

Sheriff Harris handed them a map and the address of the cabin. "Be careful. Turner is paranoid and dangerous. Approach with caution."

Emma and Sam prepared for the journey, packing supplies and making sure they had everything they needed. As they drove towards the cabin, the sense of urgency grew. They knew this was a crucial step in their investigation, but the risks were high.

The road to the cabin was narrow and winding, cutting through dense forest. They parked a distance away and continued on foot, moving quietly through the trees. The cabin came into view, a small, weathered structure surrounded by overgrown vegetation.

Emma and Sam approached cautiously, keeping an eye out for any signs of danger. They reached the cabin and knocked on the door, holding their breath as they waited.

The door creaked open, revealing a haggard man with piercing eyes. Michael Turner looked them over, his expression wary. "Who are you? What do you want?"

"We're not here to hurt you," Emma said quickly. "My name is Emma Collins, and this is Sam Johnson. We're investigating Henry Whitaker, and we need your help."

Turner's eyes narrowed. "Whitaker? What makes you think I'll help you?"

Emma held up the documents they had found. "We have evidence of his crimes. We know you used to work with him, but things went wrong. We need to bring him to justice, and you're the only one who can help us."

Turner hesitated, then stepped aside, letting them into the cabin. "You have no idea what you're getting into," he muttered as he closed the door behind them.

Inside, the cabin was sparse, with minimal furniture and signs of a solitary life. Turner gestured for them to sit at the small table, and he took a seat opposite them.

"Whitaker is dangerous," Turner began, his voice low. "He has powerful connections, people who will do anything to protect him. I tried to get out, but he wouldn't let me. That's why I'm here, hiding."

Emma leaned forward. "We need to know everything. His connections, his plans—anything that can help us stop him."

Turner sighed, rubbing his temples. "Whitaker had a network of corrupt officials, businessmen, and enforcers. He used the Alden family's resources to launder money, intimidate rivals, and expand his influence. But his greed got the better of him. He started making mistakes, and that's when I tried to leave."

"Do you have any proof?" Sam asked.

Turner nodded. "I kept records. I knew it was my insurance if things went south. They're hidden in a safe place."

Emma's heart raced. "Can you get them for us?"

Turner looked at them, his eyes filled with a mixture of fear and determination. "If I help you, you have to promise me protection. Whitaker will come after me if he finds out I'm helping you."

"We'll make sure you're safe," Emma promised. "The sheriff is already building a case. With your help, we can bring Whitaker down and protect you."

Turner nodded slowly. "Alright. The records are hidden in a storage unit on the outskirts of town. I'll give you the key and the location. But you have to be quick. If Whitaker finds out, it'll be too late."

Emma and Sam took the key and the address, thanking Turner for his help. As they left the cabin, Emma felt a renewed sense of hope. They were getting closer to the truth, but the danger was greater than ever.

Back in Pinewood, they went straight to the storage unit. The facility was deserted, adding to the sense of urgency. They found the unit and used the key to unlock it, revealing a collection of boxes and files.

Emma and Sam quickly sorted through the boxes, finding detailed records of Whitaker's activities. The evidence was overwhelming, providing a clear trail of corruption and crime.

They took the files to Sheriff Harris, who immediately began coordinating with his team to prepare for arrests. The atmosphere in the sheriff's office was tense but hopeful. They were finally ready to take action.

That night, Emma and Sam returned to their apartment, exhausted but optimistic. They had done everything they could; now it was up to the authorities to bring Whitaker to justice.

As Emma lay in bed, she thought about the journey they had been on. The whispers, the shadows, the secrets—they had all led to this moment. The truth was finally coming to light, but the fight was not over.

The next morning, Emma received a call from Sheriff Harris. "We've made the arrests," he said. "Whitaker and his associates are in custody. We've also arranged protection for Michael Turner. Thank you for your help, Emma. We couldn't have done this without you."

Emma felt a wave of relief. The nightmare was finally over. Pinewood could begin to heal, and the Alden family's legacy would be restored.

But as Emma and Sam celebrated their victory, a nagging feeling remained. The shadows of Pinewood had been deep and dark, and she couldn't shake the sense that there were still secrets waiting to be uncovered. The journey had been long and dangerous, but Emma Collins was ready for whatever came next.

Chapter 8: Dangerous Discoveries

The arrests of Henry Whitaker and his associates sent shockwaves through Pinewood. For the first time in years, the town seemed to breathe a collective sigh of relief. The story made headlines, and Emma was hailed as a hero for her relentless pursuit of the truth. But beneath the surface, Emma couldn't shake the feeling that the mystery wasn't entirely solved.

A week after the arrests, Emma sat at her desk in the Pinewood Gazette, organizing her notes for a follow-up article. She had just finished writing the piece when Sam walked over, a concerned look on his face.

"Emma, there's someone here to see you," he said quietly. "He says it's urgent."

Emma looked up, curiosity piqued. "Who is it?"

"A man named David Alden," Sam replied. "He claims to be a distant relative of the Alden family."

Emma's heart skipped a beat. A relative of the Aldens? She hadn't come across any mention of a David Alden in her research. She stood up and followed Sam to the front office, where a tall, middle-aged man with sharp features and piercing blue eyes was waiting.

"Mr. Alden?" Emma greeted him. "I'm Emma Collins. How can I help you?"

David Alden extended his hand. "Thank you for seeing me, Ms. Collins. I read about your investigation into my family's disappearance. I believe I have information that could be of interest to you."

Emma led David to a small conference room, eager to hear what he had to say. They sat down, and David took a deep breath before speaking.

"My great-uncle was Richard Alden," he began. "I grew up hearing stories about the family and their mysterious disappearance. But there's something you need to know—something that wasn't in your articles."

Emma leaned forward, her curiosity piqued. "What is it?"

David hesitated, then pulled out an old, worn notebook. "This belonged to my father, Thomas Alden. He was Richard's nephew. He kept a detailed journal of his own investigation into the family's disappearance. After reading your articles, I felt it was time to share it with you."

Emma took the notebook, her hands trembling with anticipation. She flipped through the pages, her eyes scanning the handwritten entries. The journal detailed Thomas Alden's efforts to uncover the truth, including interviews with people who had known the family and notes on suspicious activities.

"Your father was investigating the same things I was," Emma said, looking up at David. "Why didn't he come forward sooner?"

David sighed. "He tried, but every time he got close to the truth, something would happen. People would refuse to talk, evidence would disappear—it was as if someone was always one step ahead of him. He eventually gave up, but he never stopped believing that there was more to the story."

Emma's mind raced as she processed the information. "Do you think someone else was involved in the Alden family's disappearance? Someone besides Henry Whitaker?"

David nodded. "I do. My father believed there was a larger conspiracy at play, one that involved more powerful and influential people. Whitaker was just the tip of the iceberg."

Emma felt a chill run down her spine. The thought of a larger conspiracy was both terrifying and intriguing. "Do you have any idea who these people might be?"

David shook his head. "No, but I believe my father's journal holds clues that could help you find out. He was meticulous in his research, and he documented everything."

Emma thanked David for sharing the journal and promised to keep him informed of any new developments. As he left, she felt a renewed sense of determination. The mystery was far from over, and she was more determined than ever to uncover the truth.

That evening, Emma and Sam sat in her apartment, poring over Thomas Alden's journal. The entries were detailed and filled with names, dates, and locations. One name in particular stood out: Marcus Thorne, a wealthy businessman with ties to Pinewood's elite.

"Who is Marcus Thorne?" Sam asked, his brow furrowed as he read the entries.

"According to this, he's a prominent figure in Pinewood's business community," Emma replied. "But my research didn't turn up anything on him. It's like he was hiding in plain sight."

They decided to dig deeper into Marcus Thorne's background. Emma searched through public records and news archives, finding surprisingly little information about him. He had managed to keep a low profile, despite his wealth and influence.

"There's something off about this guy," Emma said, frustration evident in her voice. "He's too clean, too perfect. It's like he's erased any trace of his involvement in anything questionable."

Sam nodded. "Maybe we should pay him a visit. See if we can get any answers."

The next morning, Emma and Sam drove to Thorne's estate, a sprawling mansion on the outskirts of Pinewood. The property was heavily guarded, and they knew they had to be careful. They parked a distance away and approached the gates on foot.

As they reached the entrance, a security guard stepped forward, blocking their path. "Can I help you?" he asked, his tone polite but firm.

"We're here to see Mr. Thorne," Emma said, trying to sound confident. "We're journalists from the Pinewood Gazette, and we have some questions about his business dealings."

The guard's expression didn't change. "Mr. Thorne is a busy man. Do you have an appointment?"

Emma shook her head. "No, but it's urgent. Please, just tell him we're here."

The guard hesitated, then spoke into his radio. After a moment, he nodded. "Wait here."

Emma and Sam exchanged nervous glances as they waited. After what felt like an eternity, the guard returned. "Mr. Thorne will see you. Follow me."

They followed the guard through the gates and up the long driveway to the mansion. The interior was opulent, filled with expensive art and luxurious furnishings. They were led to a large study, where Marcus Thorne sat behind a massive desk, his piercing gaze fixed on them.

"Mr. Thorne," Emma began, trying to steady her nerves. "Thank you for seeing us. We have some questions about your connections to the Alden family and Henry Whitaker."

Thorne's expression remained impassive. "The Alden family? That was a long time ago. I'm not sure how I can help you."

Emma took a deep breath. "We have reason to believe you were involved in their disappearance, and in Whitaker's illegal activities."

Thorne's eyes narrowed. "Those are serious accusations, Ms. Collins. Do you have any proof?"

Emma hesitated, then pulled out Thomas Alden's journal. "This journal documents your connections to Whitaker and the Aldens. We believe there's a larger conspiracy at play, and you're at the center of it."

Thorne leaned back in his chair, his expression unreadable. "You have no idea what you're getting into. This isn't a game, Ms. Collins. There are powerful people involved, people who won't hesitate to protect their interests."

Emma's heart pounded, but she refused to back down. "We're not afraid. The truth needs to come out, and we won't stop until it does."

Thorne's gaze was cold and calculating. "Very well. If you want the truth, you'll have it. But be warned—once you start down this path, there's no turning back."

Emma and Sam left the mansion, their minds reeling from the encounter. Thorne's words had been chilling, but they were more determined than ever to uncover the truth. The stakes were higher than they had imagined, but they were ready to face whatever dangers lay ahead.

Back at the Pinewood Gazette, they reviewed the information they had gathered. Thorne's connections to Whitaker were clear, but there were still many unanswered questions. They decided to follow up on some of the names mentioned in Thomas Alden's journal, hoping to find more leads.

As they delved deeper, they uncovered a network of corruption and deceit that reached far beyond Pinewood. Influential figures, both locally and nationally, were implicated in the conspiracy. It was a web of lies and betrayal, and Emma knew they were only scratching the surface.

The next few days were a blur of research and interviews. They spoke to former associates of Thorne and Whitaker, each revealing more pieces of the puzzle. The more they uncovered, the more dangerous the situation became.

One night, as Emma was working late at the Gazette, she received a call from an unknown number. She answered hesitantly, her heart pounding in her chest.

"Ms. Collins," a voice said, low and urgent. "You need to stop. You're in over your head."

"Who is this?" Emma demanded, her voice trembling.

"Someone who knows the truth," the voice replied. "You're getting too close. If you don't back off, there will be consequences."

The line went dead, and Emma stared at the phone, her mind racing. The threat was real, and she knew she had to be careful. But she also knew she couldn't stop now. The truth was within their grasp, and she was determined to see it through.

Emma and Sam doubled their efforts, working tirelessly to piece together the evidence. They knew time was running out, and the danger was growing. But they also knew they had to keep going. The whispers in the night, the shadows that followed them—they were all signs that they were on the right track.

As they prepared to confront Marcus Thorne again, Emma couldn't help but feel a sense of foreboding. The darkness was closing in, and the stakes were higher than ever. But she was ready. The truth needed to come out, and she would stop at nothing to uncover it.

The journey was far from over, and the dangers were greater than ever. But Emma Collins was ready to face whatever lay ahead. The secrets of Pinewood were waiting to be revealed, and she was determined to bring them to light, no matter the cost.

Chapter 9: The Key to the Puzzle

The atmosphere in Pinewood had grown tense since the arrests of Henry Whitaker and his associates. Emma and Sam felt the weight of the town's eyes on them, some grateful, others suspicious. The mysterious warning call still echoed in Emma's mind, but it only fueled her determination. They were closing in on the truth, and there was no turning back now.

Emma and Sam decided it was time to confront Marcus Thorne with their latest findings. They had uncovered more evidence linking him to Whitaker's illegal activities and the Alden family's disappearance. Thorne had hinted at a larger conspiracy, and they needed him to reveal the full extent of it.

They drove to Thorne's estate once again, this time armed with more evidence and a steely resolve. As they approached the gates, Emma's phone buzzed. It was Sheriff Harris.

"Emma, be careful," he warned. "We have reason to believe Thorne is more dangerous than we thought. Make sure you're not alone."

Emma assured the sheriff they would be cautious and ended the call. She and Sam exchanged a glance, both understanding the risks but determined to see this through.

The same security guard let them in, and they were led to Thorne's study. Marcus Thorne sat behind his massive desk, his expression unreadable as they entered. The opulent room felt colder than before, the tension palpable.

"Ms. Collins, Mr. Johnson," Thorne greeted them, his voice smooth. "Back so soon? I take it you've found more... interesting information."

Emma nodded, placing a folder on Thorne's desk. "We've uncovered more evidence of your involvement in Whitaker's activities and the Alden family's disappearance. We know there's a larger conspiracy at play, and we need you to tell us everything."

Thorne's eyes flickered with something—anger, fear, or perhaps amusement. "You're persistent, I'll give you that. But you're treading dangerous waters."

Emma took a deep breath. "We know about your connections to organized crime, the threats to the Alden family, and your efforts to cover it all up. The truth will come out, Mr. Thorne, whether you help us or not."

Thorne leaned back, his gaze fixed on Emma. "You think you can handle the truth? Very well. But understand this: once you know, there's no going back."

Emma and Sam remained silent, waiting for Thorne to continue.

"Henry Whitaker was just a pawn," Thorne began. "A useful one, but a pawn nonetheless. The real power lies with a group of influential figures—politicians, businessmen, people who control the strings behind the scenes. Whitaker's mistake was trying to outmaneuver them. He got greedy, and that sealed his fate."

Thorne paused, studying their reactions. "Richard Alden discovered Whitaker's involvement with this group. He threatened to expose them, and that's when things turned deadly. The threats, the intimidation—it was all orchestrated to silence him. When that didn't work, they decided to eliminate the Aldens."

Emma's heart pounded. "Who are these people? Can you name them?"

Thorne's expression darkened. "I can, but it won't do you any good. They're protected, untouchable. Going after them is a death sentence."

Sam leaned forward. "We need those names, Thorne. We need to bring them to justice."

Thorne sighed, then opened a drawer in his desk, pulling out a piece of paper. "These are some of the key players. But be warned—they won't go down without a fight."

Emma took the paper, her hands trembling. The list contained names she recognized—prominent figures in politics and business. It was a web of corruption and deceit that reached far beyond Pinewood.

As they left Thorne's estate, Emma and Sam felt a mixture of triumph and dread. They had the names, but they also understood the enormity of the task ahead. Bringing these powerful individuals to justice would be dangerous, possibly deadly.

Back at the Pinewood Gazette, Emma and Sam shared their findings with Sheriff Harris. The sheriff's expression was grave as he reviewed the names.

"This is big," he said. "Bigger than anything we've dealt with before. We'll need to involve federal authorities, and even then, it's going to be a battle."

Emma nodded. "We're ready for it. Whatever it takes to bring these people down."

Sheriff Harris began coordinating with federal agents, setting the wheels in motion for a larger investigation. Meanwhile, Emma and Sam continued to gather more evidence, interviewing witnesses and tracking down leads.

The days that followed were a blur of activity. Emma barely slept, her mind racing with the details of the conspiracy. The danger was ever-present, but so was her determination. She knew they were on the right path, and she was willing to risk everything for the truth.

One evening, as Emma and Sam were going over their notes in the office, they heard a noise outside. Emma's heart raced as she peered through the window, seeing a figure standing in the shadows. She couldn't make out the face, but the presence was menacing.

"We need to be careful," Sam said, his voice low. "They're watching us."

Emma nodded, her resolve hardening. "Let them watch. We're not backing down."

As the investigation progressed, the pressure mounted. They received more threats, anonymous calls warning them to stop. But each threat only strengthened their resolve.

One night, Emma was working late at the Gazette when her phone buzzed with a message. It was from an unknown number, containing only a single word: "Enough."

Emma felt a chill run down her spine. She showed the message to Sam, who frowned.

"They're getting desperate," he said. "We must be getting close."

Emma nodded. "We need to be careful, but we can't stop now. We're too close to the truth."

The next day, Emma received a call from one of the federal agents working with Sheriff Harris. "We've identified a safe house for you and Mr. Johnson. It's best you go there while we make the final preparations for the arrests."

Emma agreed, understanding the necessity of caution. She and Sam packed their essentials and left for the safe house, their minds still focused on the task at hand.

The safe house was a small, secluded cabin, surrounded by trees and far from any prying eyes. It felt both secure and isolating, a place where they could gather their thoughts and prepare for the final push.

As they settled in, Emma reviewed their findings, making sure everything was in order. They had come so far, and the end was in sight. But she knew the most dangerous part was still ahead.

One evening, as they were discussing their next steps, there was a knock at the door. Emma and Sam exchanged a glance, their hands instinctively reaching for their phones.

"Who is it?" Emma called out.

"It's David Alden," came the reply. "I have more information for you."

Emma hesitated, then opened the door. David Alden stood there, looking anxious. He stepped inside, glancing around nervously.

"I found something else in my father's belongings," David said, handing Emma a small, leather-bound book. "It's a record of meetings between the key players in the conspiracy. My father managed to get his hands on it before he disappeared."

Emma opened the book, her eyes widening as she scanned the pages. It contained detailed notes on the meetings, including dates, locations, and the topics discussed. It was the final piece of the puzzle.

"This is incredible," Emma said, her voice filled with awe. "Thank you, David. This could be the key to bringing them down."

David nodded, his expression somber. "Be careful. These people are dangerous. They won't go down without a fight."

Emma and Sam spent the next few days in the safe house, compiling their evidence and preparing for the final confrontation. The federal agents and Sheriff Harris were coordinating the arrests, and the tension was palpable.

On the day of the operation, Emma and Sam watched from the safe house as the authorities moved in. It was a coordinated effort, with agents arresting key figures in the conspiracy across multiple locations. The news spread quickly, and Pinewood was in shock.

As the dust settled, Emma and Sam were brought in to give their statements. The evidence they had gathered, along with the information from David Alden, was enough to secure convictions for the conspirators.

The town of Pinewood began to heal, its dark secrets finally brought to light. Emma and Sam were hailed as heroes, their relentless pursuit of the truth having brought justice to the Alden family and exposed the corruption that had plagued the town for so long.

In the aftermath, Emma reflected on the journey they had been on. It had been a dangerous and arduous path, but the truth had prevailed. The shadows of Pinewood had been dispelled, and the town could finally move forward.

As Emma sat at her desk, writing the final article about the case, she felt a sense of closure. The whispers in the night were gone, replaced by the promise of a brighter future. The key to the puzzle had been found, and the truth had set Pinewood free.

Chapter 10: A Web of Lies

The days following the arrests of Marcus Thorne and his associates were a whirlwind of activity. Pinewood was abuzz with news of the conspiracy, and Emma and Sam found themselves at the center of it all. The town's atmosphere shifted from one of tension and fear to a cautious optimism as people began to believe that justice had finally been served.

Despite the outward calm, Emma knew there was still work to be done. The names on the list Marcus Thorne had given them suggested a web of corruption that reached far beyond Pinewood. Emma and Sam decided to follow up on these leads, determined to expose the full extent of the conspiracy.

One morning, Emma sat at her desk, pouring over the list of names. She had been researching each individual, trying to find connections that would unravel the network of lies and deceit. Sam walked in, carrying two cups of coffee.

"Find anything interesting?" he asked, setting one of the cups in front of her.

Emma took a sip, savoring the warmth. "A few things. Look at this," she said, pointing to one name in particular. "Michael Harper. He's a high-profile lawyer with connections to several of the people we've been investigating. It seems he's been representing some pretty shady clients over the years."

Sam leaned over to look at the information Emma had compiled. "Think he's part of the conspiracy?"

"Definitely," Emma replied. "But we need proof. Let's see if we can find someone who's worked with him and might be willing to talk."

They spent the rest of the day making calls and following leads. Eventually, they found a former employee of Harper's law firm who was willing to meet with them. The next morning, Emma and Sam drove to a small café on the outskirts of Pinewood, where they had arranged to meet the informant.

The café was quiet, with only a few patrons scattered around. Emma and Sam took a seat in a corner booth, scanning the room for their contact. A few minutes later, a nervous-looking man in his mid-forties walked in, glancing around before making his way to their table.

"Mr. Johnson?" Emma greeted him. "Thank you for meeting with us."

The man nodded, sitting down and fidgeting with his coffee cup. "Call me Peter. I'm not sure how much help I can be, but I couldn't stay silent any longer."

"We appreciate your willingness to talk," Sam said, leaning forward. "What can you tell us about Michael Harper and his connections to the people we're investigating?"

Peter took a deep breath. "Harper is a master manipulator. He has connections in politics, business, and law enforcement. He uses these connections to protect his clients and himself. Over the years, I saw him do things that were... unethical, to say the least. But I never had any concrete proof, just suspicions."

"Can you give us any specific examples?" Emma asked.

Peter nodded. "There was one case in particular. Harper represented a businessman who was accused of embezzling millions. The evidence against him was overwhelming, but somehow, Harper managed to get the charges dropped. Later, I found out that he had bribed a key witness and manipulated evidence to ensure his client walked free."

Emma felt a surge of anger. "And this businessman—do you know if he had any connections to Marcus Thorne or Henry Whitaker?"

Peter hesitated, then nodded. "Yes. He was a close associate of Thorne's. They were both part of the same network."

Emma and Sam exchanged a glance. This was the connection they had been looking for.

"Peter, would you be willing to testify about what you know?" Sam asked.

Peter looked down at his hands, then back up at them. "I'm scared. These people are powerful. But if it means bringing them to justice, then yes, I'll testify."

Emma and Sam thanked Peter for his bravery and assured him they would do everything in their power to protect him. As they left the café, Emma felt a renewed sense of determination. They were getting closer to exposing the full extent of the conspiracy.

Back at the Pinewood Gazette, Emma and Sam began compiling their evidence against Michael Harper. They reached out to other former employees of Harper's law firm, gathering more testimonies and building a solid case. They also worked closely with federal agents, ensuring every piece of evidence was documented and verified.

As the investigation progressed, they uncovered more connections between Harper and other key figures in the conspiracy. It was a web of lies and deceit that spanned multiple states and involved high-ranking officials in politics, law enforcement, and business.

One evening, as Emma was working late, she received an email from an anonymous source. The subject line read: "Proof." She opened the email, her heart racing as she scanned the contents. It contained a series of documents detailing illegal transactions, bribes, and correspondence between Harper and various conspirators.

Emma quickly forwarded the email to Sam and Sheriff Harris, then printed out the documents for their files. This was the breakthrough they needed. The evidence was irrefutable, and it would help bring down the entire network.

The next day, Emma and Sam met with Sheriff Harris and the federal agents to discuss their findings. The atmosphere in the room was tense but hopeful. They reviewed the evidence, mapping out the connections and planning their next steps.

"We have enough to move forward," one of the federal agents said. "This is going to be a major operation, but with this evidence, we can secure warrants and make arrests."

Sheriff Harris nodded. "We need to move quickly. If Harper or any of his associates get wind of this, they could destroy evidence or flee."

The team spent the next few days coordinating the operation, ensuring every detail was covered. Emma and Sam continued to gather information, working tirelessly to ensure they had everything they needed.

On the day of the operation, Emma and Sam watched anxiously as federal agents moved in to arrest Michael Harper and his associates. It was a coordinated effort, with simultaneous raids in multiple locations. The news spread quickly, and Pinewood was once again in the spotlight.

As the arrests were made, Emma felt a mix of relief and triumph. They had done it. The web of lies had been exposed, and the conspirators were finally facing justice.

Back at the Gazette, Emma and Sam wrote their final article on the case, detailing the investigation and the arrests. The story was a sensation, and the town of Pinewood began to heal from the dark legacy of the Alden family's disappearance.

In the weeks that followed, Emma and Sam continued to work with federal agents, providing testimonies and ensuring the prosecution had all the evidence they needed. The trials were long and arduous, but in the end, justice was served.

As Emma sat at her desk, reflecting on the journey they had been on, she felt a sense of closure. The truth had prevailed, and Pinewood was finally free from the shadows that had haunted it for so long.

The web of lies had been unraveled, and the town could move forward with a renewed sense of hope. Emma knew there would always be more stories to uncover, more mysteries to solve, but for now, she was content knowing they had made a difference.

Emma Collins and Sam Johnson had faced danger, uncovered secrets, and brought justice to Pinewood. Their relentless pursuit of the truth had changed the town forever, and they were ready for whatever challenges lay ahead.

Chapter 11: A Friend's Betrayal

The dust from the arrests was still settling, and Pinewood was beginning to regain a sense of normalcy. Emma and Sam were hailed as heroes, but the accolades did little to soothe Emma's lingering unease. Despite the arrests and the comprehensive investigation, there was a nagging feeling that something was still amiss.

Emma was working late at the Pinewood Gazette one evening when her phone rang. It was David Alden. "Emma, we need to talk. Can you meet me at the old train station in an hour?"

"Sure, David," Emma replied, sensing the urgency in his voice. "I'll be there."

Emma quickly gathered her things and left the office, her mind racing with questions. What could David have discovered? As she drove to the train station, she couldn't shake the feeling that this meeting would bring even more revelations.

The old train station was dimly lit and deserted, casting eerie shadows on the platform. Emma spotted David near the entrance, his expression tense.

"David, what's going on?" Emma asked as she approached him.

"I've been digging through more of my father's things," David said, his voice low. "I found something you need to see."

He handed her a folder filled with documents. Emma quickly scanned the pages, her eyes widening as she realized what she was looking at. The documents detailed a secret alliance between several high-profile individuals, some of whom were not yet implicated in the conspiracy.

"These names... they weren't on the original list," Emma said, her voice trembling.

David nodded. "Exactly. I think there are more people involved, people who managed to stay under the radar. We need to expose them before they can cover their tracks."

Emma felt a surge of determination. "Let's get back to the Gazette. We need to go through these documents carefully."

They drove back to the office, their minds racing with the implications of their discovery. As they pored over the documents, a clearer picture began to emerge. This new information connected the dots between individuals who had managed to evade suspicion, revealing a broader network of corruption.

"We need to tell Sheriff Harris," Emma said, her voice firm. "This changes everything."

David agreed, and they quickly contacted the sheriff. He arrived at the Gazette within the hour, his expression serious as he reviewed the new evidence.

"This is significant," Sheriff Harris said. "We need to act quickly before these individuals realize we're onto them."

As the sheriff coordinated with federal agents to expand the investigation, Emma and Sam continued to dig deeper. They knew they were running out of time and that the stakes were higher than ever.

One evening, as Emma was leaving the office, she received a call from an unknown number. She hesitated, then answered.

"Emma Collins?" a familiar voice said.

"Who is this?" Emma asked, her heart pounding.

"It's Michael Turner. We need to talk."

Emma was taken aback. "Turner? How did you get this number?"

"Never mind that," Turner replied. "I have information you need to hear, but we can't talk over the phone. Meet me at the abandoned warehouse on Maple Street in an hour."

Emma hesitated, then agreed. She knew the risks but felt she couldn't pass up the opportunity for more information. She called Sam, asking him to meet her at the warehouse for backup.

The warehouse was dark and foreboding, its windows shattered and its walls covered in graffiti. Emma and Sam arrived together, their flashlights cutting through the darkness.

"Turner?" Emma called out, her voice echoing in the empty space.

"Over here," a voice replied from the shadows.

Michael Turner stepped into the light, his face gaunt and his eyes filled with fear. "I didn't know who else to turn to," he said, his voice trembling. "They're onto me."

"Who?" Sam asked, his eyes scanning the area for any signs of danger.

"The people behind the conspiracy," Turner replied. "I overheard a conversation—they know you're getting close. They have someone on the inside, someone feeding them information."

Emma felt a chill run down her spine. "Who? Who's the mole?"

Turner hesitated, then looked directly at Emma. "It's someone you trust. Someone close to you."

Emma's mind raced. Who could it be? She thought about everyone involved in the investigation, her heart sinking as she realized the implications.

"Who is it, Turner?" Sam demanded.

Turner opened his mouth to answer, but before he could speak, a gunshot rang out. Turner collapsed to the ground, blood pooling around him.

"Get down!" Sam shouted, pulling Emma behind a stack of crates.

Emma's heart pounded as she tried to make sense of what had just happened. Someone was trying to silence Turner, and now they were in danger too.

"Stay low," Sam whispered. "We need to get out of here."

They moved cautiously, using the crates for cover as they made their way to the exit. Another gunshot rang out, hitting the crate just inches from Emma's head. She stifled a scream, her heart racing with fear.

"We're almost there," Sam said, his voice steady despite the danger.

They reached the door and burst outside, running to their car. Sam drove away quickly, leaving the warehouse behind. Emma looked back, her mind racing with questions and fear.

"Who do you think the mole is?" Sam asked, his grip tight on the steering wheel.

"I don't know," Emma replied, her voice shaking. "But we need to find out before they can do more damage."

Back at the safe house, Emma and Sam contacted Sheriff Harris and informed him of what had happened. The sheriff was shocked but promised to take immediate action to root out the mole.

"We'll get to the bottom of this," Sheriff Harris assured them. "But you both need to be careful. Whoever this is, they won't stop until you're silenced."

Emma and Sam spent the next few days working from the safe house, their trust shaken but their resolve stronger than ever. They reviewed their notes, trying to identify anyone who might have had access to their information.

One name kept coming up—someone they had never suspected but who had been involved in the investigation from the beginning. Emma's heart sank as she realized who it was.

"We need to confront them," Emma said, her voice firm. "But we have to be careful."

They arranged a meeting with the person they suspected, a close friend who had been by their side throughout the investigation. The meeting was tense, the air thick with suspicion and fear.

As they confronted their friend, the truth slowly came to light. Betrayal, fear, and desperation had driven their actions, but the damage had been done.

Emma felt a mix of anger and sadness as she realized the extent of the betrayal. They had trusted this person, relied on them, and now everything was in jeopardy.

"We need to go to Sheriff Harris," Emma said, her voice steady despite the turmoil inside. "We can't let this stop us."

Their friend agreed to come clean, and together they went to the sheriff's office. The atmosphere was tense as their friend confessed, revealing the full extent of their involvement and the information they had passed on.

Sheriff Harris was furious but focused. "We'll deal with this," he said. "But you need to stay safe. The people behind this are still out there, and they won't stop until they get what they want."

Emma and Sam left the sheriff's office, their minds racing with the implications of the betrayal. They had come so far, uncovered so much, but now they faced an even greater challenge.

As they drove back to the safe house, Emma felt a renewed sense of determination. They would uncover the full extent of the conspiracy, expose the remaining players, and bring justice to Pinewood. The path ahead was dangerous, but they were ready to face whatever came their way.

The truth was out there, waiting to be uncovered, and Emma Collins would not rest until it was brought to light. The shadows of Pinewood were deep and dark, but she was ready to face them head-on, no matter the cost.

Chapter 12: Race Against Time

The revelation of their friend's betrayal had shaken Emma and Sam, but it also fueled their determination. They knew they were running out of time. The people behind the conspiracy were still out there, watching, waiting. Emma and Sam were more resolved than ever to expose the full extent of the corruption.

Emma decided it was time to take a more aggressive approach. They needed to gather the remaining pieces of evidence quickly and ensure their safety. She reached out to David Alden and Sheriff Harris, coordinating their next steps.

"We need to move fast," Emma said during a meeting at the safe house. "The longer we wait, the more time they have to cover their tracks."

Sheriff Harris nodded. "We'll increase security around you both. The federal agents are still working on the case, but we need more concrete evidence to make the final arrests."

David Alden, looking more determined than ever, spoke up. "I've been going through more of my father's files. I think there's a hidden safe in the Alden mansion that contains crucial documents. It's risky, but it might be our last chance."

Emma agreed. "We need to go there. Sam and I will retrieve the documents. Sheriff, can you provide us with backup?"

"I'll send a team with you," Sheriff Harris said. "But be prepared for anything."

That evening, Emma and Sam, accompanied by a team of deputies, made their way to the Alden mansion. The house stood silent and imposing, a reminder of the secrets it had guarded for so long. As they approached, Emma's heart raced with a mix of fear and anticipation.

Inside the mansion, they moved quickly and quietly. David had provided them with the location of the hidden safe, a concealed panel behind a bookshelf in Richard Alden's study. Emma and Sam worked together to move the heavy furniture and reveal the hidden compartment.

Emma's hands trembled as she entered the combination David had given her. The safe clicked open, revealing a stack of documents, photographs, and a small leather-bound diary. Emma carefully took out the contents, her eyes scanning the information.

"These are it," she whispered to Sam. "These are the final pieces we need."

As they gathered the documents, Emma heard a noise from upstairs. Her heart pounded. They weren't alone.

"Someone's here," Sam whispered, his eyes wide with alarm.

The deputies, alerted by the noise, moved to secure the perimeter. Emma and Sam remained hidden, clutching the documents tightly. They could hear footsteps approaching, the creak of the old floorboards growing louder.

A figure appeared at the top of the stairs, their face obscured by shadows. Emma recognized the silhouette—it was Marcus Thorne.

"Well, well," Thorne said, his voice dripping with contempt. "I see you've found my little secret."

Emma's heart raced. Thorne had somehow managed to avoid arrest and had come to the mansion, likely to destroy the very evidence they had found.

"Drop the documents," Thorne commanded, his hand reaching into his coat.

Before Emma or Sam could react, the deputies moved in, their guns trained on Thorne. "Freeze!" one of them shouted. "Put your hands up!"

Thorne hesitated, then slowly raised his hands. Emma felt a rush of relief as the deputies secured Thorne and ensured the house was safe.

"We've got him," one of the deputies said. "You're safe now."

Emma and Sam emerged from their hiding spot, clutching the documents tightly. They knew this was only part of the battle, but it was a significant victory.

Back at the safe house, Emma, Sam, and Sheriff Harris reviewed the documents. They contained detailed records of illegal transactions, correspondences between key conspirators, and evidence linking high-profile individuals to the corruption.

"This is it," Emma said, her voice filled with determination. "We have everything we need."

Sheriff Harris nodded. "We'll take this to the federal agents immediately. They can move forward with the final arrests."

The following days were a blur of activity as federal agents coordinated the arrests of the remaining conspirators. Emma and Sam watched as the news unfolded, feeling a mix of relief and triumph.

But Emma knew their work wasn't over. There were still loose ends to tie up, questions to answer, and a town to help rebuild. She and Sam continued their investigation, ensuring that every aspect of the conspiracy was exposed.

One morning, as Emma was working on her final article for the Pinewood Gazette, she received a call from David Alden.

"Emma," David said, his voice filled with gratitude. "I can't thank you enough for everything you've done. My family can finally rest in peace."

Emma felt a surge of emotion. "Thank you, David. We couldn't have done it without your help. Pinewood owes you and your father a great debt."

David paused, then said, "There's one more thing. I found another diary in my father's belongings. It details the last days before the Alden family's disappearance. I think it will give you the closure you need."

Emma agreed to meet David and retrieve the diary. As she read through the final entries, she felt a sense of peace. Richard Alden had fought valiantly to protect his family and expose the truth. His legacy would live on through the justice they had achieved.

In the weeks that followed, Emma and Sam continued their work, helping Pinewood heal from the dark shadow that had loomed over it for so long. The town began to rebuild, its residents finding hope and strength in the wake of the revelations.

One evening, as Emma sat on her porch, reflecting on the journey they had been on, Sam joined her, a look of contentment on his face.

"We did it," Sam said, sitting down beside her. "We brought justice to Pinewood."

Emma nodded, a smile spreading across her face. "Yes, we did. And we couldn't have done it without each other."

As the sun set over Pinewood, Emma felt a sense of closure. The truth had prevailed, and the town could finally move forward. There would always be more stories to uncover, more mysteries to solve, but for now, she was content knowing they had made a difference.

Emma Collins and Sam Johnson had faced danger, uncovered secrets, and brought justice to Pinewood. Their relentless pursuit of the truth had changed the town forever, and they were ready for whatever challenges lay ahead.

Chapter 13: The Final Confrontation

The sense of peace in Pinewood was a hard-earned victory, but Emma knew there was still one last loose end to tie up: the final confrontation with the mastermind behind the conspiracy. As the dust settled from the recent arrests, new information came to light, suggesting that a powerful figure had orchestrated the entire operation from the shadows.

Emma, Sam, and Sheriff Harris met in the Gazette's conference room, reviewing the latest intel. The name that surfaced was one that none of them had expected: Senator Charles Whitmore, a respected politician with a clean public image but a hidden connection to the criminal network they had exposed.

"We can't let this go," Emma said, her voice firm. "Senator Whitmore needs to be held accountable."

Sheriff Harris nodded. "Agreed. But going after a sitting senator is going to be tough. We'll need undeniable proof and a solid plan."

Emma and Sam spent the next few days gathering evidence, tracing Whitmore's connections to the conspiracy. They uncovered financial records, correspondences, and testimonies linking him to the criminal activities that had plagued Pinewood. Each piece of evidence painted a damning picture of Whitmore's involvement.

As they compiled their findings, Emma received a call from an anonymous source claiming to have crucial information about Whitmore. The source agreed to meet them at a secluded cabin outside Pinewood. Despite the risks, Emma and Sam decided to take the chance, hoping it would provide the final piece of the puzzle.

The drive to the cabin was tense. They parked a short distance away and approached the cabin cautiously. Inside, they found a man in his fifties, his face lined with worry.

"Thank you for meeting us," Emma said. "What do you have for us?"

The man, who introduced himself as John, handed Emma a flash drive. "This contains recordings of conversations between Whitmore and key members of the conspiracy. It's everything you need to bring him down."

Emma's heart raced as she accepted the flash drive. "Why are you giving us this?"

John sighed. "I used to work for Whitmore. When I realized what he was involved in, I tried to get out. But it's not that easy. This is my way of making things right."

They thanked John and quickly left the cabin, their minds focused on the new evidence. Back at the Gazette, they reviewed the recordings, confirming the incriminating content. It was the final nail in Whitmore's coffin.

The next morning, Emma and Sam met with Sheriff Harris and the federal agents to plan the arrest. They knew they had to move quickly and carefully, given Whitmore's high profile and powerful connections.

As they prepared to confront Whitmore, Emma couldn't shake the feeling of impending danger. They were taking on one of the most powerful men in the state, and the risks were enormous.

The day of the arrest arrived. Emma, Sam, and the federal agents gathered at Whitmore's estate, ready to execute their plan. The tension was palpable as they approached the front door.

"Stay alert," Sheriff Harris whispered. "This could get messy."

They knocked on the door, and after a moment, Senator Whitmore himself answered. His expression shifted from surprise to anger as he saw the badges and the determined looks on their faces.

"Senator Whitmore," one of the agents said, "we have a warrant for your arrest. You are being charged with conspiracy, corruption, and numerous other crimes."

Whitmore's face turned pale, but he quickly composed himself. "This is outrageous," he snarled. "You have no idea who you're dealing with."

Emma stepped forward, holding up the flash drive. "We know exactly who we're dealing with. And we have all the evidence we need to prove it."

Whitmore's eyes narrowed, and for a moment, Emma saw the true depth of his ruthlessness. "You'll regret this," he hissed.

The agents moved in, handcuffing Whitmore and leading him away. As they did, Emma felt a wave of relief wash over her. The mastermind had been exposed, and justice was finally within reach.

Back at the Gazette, Emma and Sam watched the news coverage of Whitmore's arrest. The story quickly became a national sensation, and Pinewood was once again thrust into the spotlight. This time, however, it was a story of triumph, of a small town standing up to corruption and winning.

In the days that followed, Emma and Sam worked tirelessly to ensure the story was told accurately and thoroughly. They interviewed witnesses, gathered statements, and wrote a comprehensive account of the investigation and its outcome.

One evening, as they were wrapping up their work, Emma received a call from David Alden. "Emma, I just wanted to thank you again. My family can finally rest in peace, thanks to you and Sam."

Emma smiled, feeling a sense of fulfillment. "Thank you, David. We couldn't have done it without your help."

After the call, Emma and Sam sat on the porch of the Gazette, watching the sun set over Pinewood. The town had been through so much, but it had emerged stronger and more resilient.

"We did it," Sam said, breaking the silence. "We really did it."

Emma nodded, her heart full of pride and relief. "Yes, we did. And Pinewood is better for it."

As the stars began to twinkle in the night sky, Emma felt a deep sense of peace. The journey had been long and fraught with danger, but they had uncovered the truth and brought justice to those who had been wronged.

The town of Pinewood could finally move forward, free from the shadows of its past. And as for Emma and Sam, they knew there would always be more stories to uncover, more mysteries to solve. But for now, they were content knowing they had made a difference.

The final confrontation had been won, and the truth had prevailed. Pinewood was free, and Emma Collins and Sam Johnson were ready for whatever challenges lay ahead.

Chapter 14: Truth Revealed

The arrest of Senator Charles Whitmore marked a turning point for Pinewood. The town, once shrouded in secrets and corruption, was now on a path to healing and renewal. The story of the conspiracy, its unraveling, and the heroes who had brought it to light became a beacon of hope for many.

Emma and Sam's relentless pursuit of the truth had not only exposed the dark underbelly of their town but also inspired a new sense of community and justice. Their work, however, was far from over. The investigation had left behind a tangled web of loose ends, and they were determined to tie them up.

In the weeks following Whitmore's arrest, Emma and Sam continued to dig deeper into the senator's dealings. They uncovered more connections, leading to additional arrests and further solidifying the case against the entire network of conspirators. The evidence was overwhelming, and the trials that followed were swift and decisive.

One morning, Emma received a call from the federal agent who had been leading the investigation. "Emma, we've got a lead on one of Whitmore's key associates, someone who managed to slip through the cracks. We need your help to track him down."

Emma agreed without hesitation. The pursuit of justice was far from over, and she knew that every piece of the puzzle was crucial. She and Sam met with the agent to discuss their plan.

The lead pointed to a remote cabin in the mountains, a place where the associate, a man named Vincent Blackwood, was believed to be hiding. Emma and Sam, along with a team of federal agents, prepared for the journey.

The drive to the mountains was long and arduous. The narrow, winding roads were treacherous, but Emma's resolve never wavered. She knew that finding Blackwood was essential to ensuring that the full extent of the conspiracy was revealed.

As they approached the cabin, the team moved cautiously, aware of the potential danger. The cabin was isolated, surrounded by dense forest. The air was thick with tension as they made their way to the front door.

Emma knocked, her heart pounding in her chest. There was no answer. She nodded to the agents, who moved in to breach the door. With a swift motion, they entered the cabin, their guns drawn.

Inside, the cabin was dark and cluttered. Emma's flashlight swept across the room, revealing signs of a hurried departure. Papers were strewn across the floor, and the faint smell of smoke lingered in the air.

"He's gone," one of the agents said, his voice tense. "But he left in a hurry. We might still have a chance to catch him."

Emma and Sam searched the cabin, gathering any documents and evidence they could find. Among the chaos, Emma discovered a map with marked locations, one of which was circled in red.

"This might be where he's headed," Emma said, showing the map to the lead agent. "We need to move fast."

The team quickly regrouped and set off towards the marked location. The pursuit was intense, the urgency palpable. As they neared the location, they spotted a figure moving through the trees.

"There he is!" Sam shouted, pointing towards the fleeing man.

The agents sprang into action, chasing after Blackwood. Emma and Sam followed, their adrenaline pumping. The chase was relentless, the terrain rough and unforgiving. But they were determined not to let him escape.

Blackwood stumbled, and the agents closed in, surrounding him. He raised his hands in surrender, breathing heavily.

"It's over, Blackwood," the lead agent said. "You're under arrest."

As the agents secured Blackwood and led him away, Emma felt a wave of relief. Another piece of the puzzle had fallen into place, bringing them closer to complete justice.

Back in Pinewood, Emma and Sam reviewed the evidence they had gathered from the cabin. It contained crucial information about the remaining members of the conspiracy and their plans. The final threads were being woven together, revealing the full scope of the corruption.

The trials that followed were a testament to the power of perseverance and justice. One by one, the remaining conspirators were convicted, their influence dismantled. The story of Pinewood's redemption spread far and wide, inspiring others to stand up against corruption and fight for the truth.

As the town began to rebuild, Emma and Sam received numerous accolades and recognition for their work. They were invited to speak at conferences, their story shared in newspapers and on television. But through it all, they remained focused on their mission.

One evening, as they sat on the porch of the Gazette, watching the sun set over Pinewood, Sam turned to Emma. "We did it, Emma. We brought them all to justice."

Emma nodded, a smile spreading across her face. "Yes, we did. But it wasn't just us. It was the people of Pinewood, the federal agents, David Alden—everyone who believed in the truth."

As the stars began to twinkle in the night sky, Emma felt a deep sense of fulfillment. The journey had been long and fraught with danger, but they had uncovered the truth and brought justice to those who had been wronged.

The town of Pinewood had emerged from the shadows, stronger and more resilient. And for Emma Collins and Sam Johnson, there would always be more stories to uncover, more mysteries to solve. But for now, they were content knowing they had made a difference.

The truth had been revealed, and Pinewood was finally free. Emma and Sam were ready for whatever challenges lay ahead, confident in their ability to face them head-on.

Chapter 15: New Beginnings

The town of Pinewood was beginning to thrive again. The dark days of corruption and conspiracy seemed like a distant memory as the community came together to rebuild and move forward. The arrests and trials had brought justice and a renewed sense of hope to the town.

Emma Collins and Sam Johnson had become local heroes, their relentless pursuit of the truth earning them the admiration and respect of their fellow citizens. But with the dust settling and the immediate danger behind them, they knew it was time to think about the future.

One sunny morning, as Emma walked through the bustling town square, she couldn't help but smile at the signs of new life around her. Shops were reopening, children played in the park, and the townspeople greeted each other with a sense of camaraderie that had been missing for far too long.

As she made her way to the Pinewood Gazette, Emma felt a sense of excitement. She and Sam had decided to expand the newspaper, turning it into a regional publication that would continue to investigate and report on important stories. They wanted to ensure that the truth always had a voice.

Inside the Gazette, Sam was already at work, surrounded by stacks of papers and a flurry of activity. He looked up as Emma entered, a broad smile on his face.

"Good morning, partner," he greeted her. "Ready for another day of chasing stories?"

Emma laughed. "Always. What have we got on the docket today?"

Sam handed her a list of potential stories, ranging from local events to more significant regional issues. "I think we should start with the new community center project. It's a great story about how the town is coming together to build something positive."

Emma nodded. "Agreed. And I want to follow up on the environmental cleanup efforts at the old factory site. It's important that we keep the public informed on progress there."

As they discussed their plans, the phone rang. Emma answered, her journalistic instincts kicking in.

"Pinewood Gazette, this is Emma Collins."

"Ms. Collins, this is Agent Carter from the FBI. I wanted to thank you and Mr. Johnson again for your cooperation in the Whitmore case. Your work was instrumental in bringing those criminals to justice."

Emma felt a surge of pride. "Thank you, Agent Carter. It was a team effort. Is there something we can help you with?"

"Actually, yes," Agent Carter replied. "We have a new case that we believe might interest you. It's in the early stages, but we could use your investigative skills. Would you be interested?"

Emma's heart raced. The prospect of a new investigation was both thrilling and daunting. "Of course. Send us the details, and we'll get started right away."

As she hung up the phone, Emma turned to Sam, excitement in her eyes. "Looks like we have a new case. Agent Carter from the FBI wants our help."

Sam grinned. "Just when we thought things were settling down. I'm in. Let's show them what the Pinewood Gazette can do."

With renewed energy, Emma and Sam dove into their work. They balanced their local reporting with the new investigation, their days filled with interviews, research, and the thrill of uncovering the truth.

As the weeks passed, the Gazette's readership grew, and the paper became known for its fearless reporting and commitment to justice. Emma and Sam's reputation as investigative journalists spread, and they received tips and leads from all over the region.

One evening, after a particularly long day, Emma and Sam sat on the porch of the Gazette, reflecting on their journey. The sun set behind the mountains, casting a warm glow over the town they had fought so hard to protect.

"We've come a long way, haven't we?" Sam said, his voice filled with pride.

Emma nodded, a smile spreading across her face. "We have. And I couldn't have done it without you, Sam. We're a good team."

Sam raised his coffee mug in a toast. "To new beginnings and the truth, wherever it leads us."

Emma clinked her mug against his. "To new beginnings."

As the stars began to twinkle in the night sky, Emma felt a deep sense of peace. The journey they had been on had changed them both, forging a bond that was unbreakable. They had faced danger, uncovered secrets, and brought justice to Pinewood. And they were ready for whatever challenges lay ahead.

The town of Pinewood had emerged from the shadows, stronger and more resilient. The Pinewood Gazette was a beacon of truth and integrity, a testament to the power of perseverance and the importance of a free press.

Emma Collins and Sam Johnson had found their calling. They were more than just journalists; they were defenders of the truth, champions of justice, and voices for the voiceless. Their work had made a difference, and they knew that as long as there were stories to uncover and truths to be told, they would be there, ready to face the challenges and embrace the new beginnings that lay ahead.

As the night settled over Pinewood, Emma and Sam looked out at the town they had helped save. The future was bright, and they were ready to meet it head-on, together.

About the Author

Linda Carrol, a native of rural Biloxi, Mississippi, discovered her passion for storytelling amidst the quiet beauty of her Southern surroundings. With her closest neighbor miles away, Linda sought solace and adventure within the pages of by authors such as Rex Stout, Stephen King, and Michael Connelly.

Armed with a degree in education from Mississippi State University, Linda embarked on a fulfilling career as an elementary school teacher. However, her love for literature and her desire to ignite the imaginations of people led her down a new path.

Fueled by a deep-seated passion for literature, Linda made the bold decision to transition from teaching to writing, channeling the enchanting storytelling styles of her literary heroes into her own work. Since then, she has emerged as one of Mississippi's most prolific writers, captivating readers with her vivid imagination, Southern charm, and heartfelt narratives.

Linda's dedication to fostering a love of reading extends beyond the written page. Through workshops and community outreach programs, she continues to inspire readers to explore new worlds and discover the magic of storytelling.

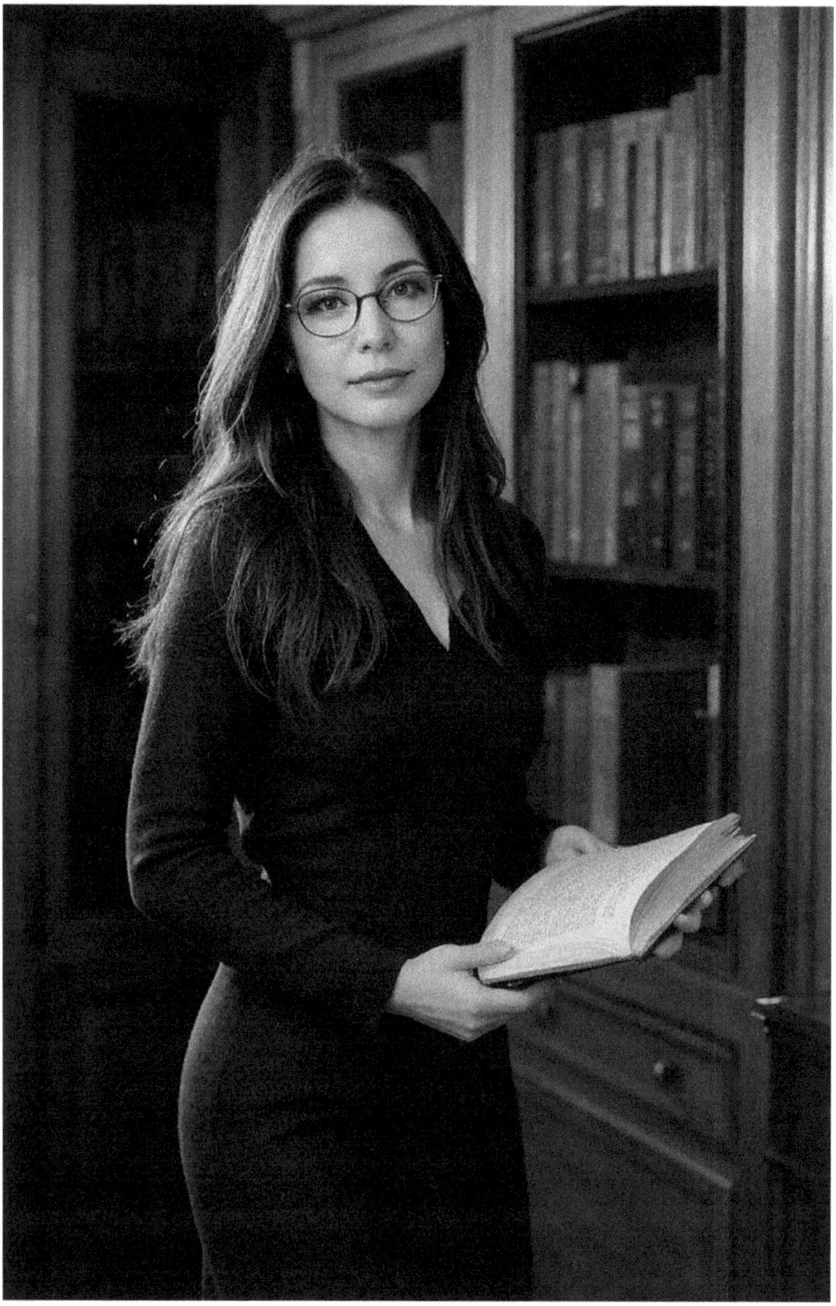

Milton Keynes UK
Ingram Content Group UK Ltd.
UKHW051448140724
445326UK00013BA/457